JAMESTOWNE'S UNCOVERED TREASURES

Judy M. Brown

The Dietz Press

To

Stan,

My Best Friend

Thanks to Jan Brown, whose creativity is a constant inspiration;

Wert Smith, whose enthusiasm, expertise, and good humor have been

unwavering; Judy Baxter, reading educator, who read the first stories and

believed them to be worthwhile; APVA staff members who are always helpful:

Ann Berry, Catherine Correll-Walls, Michael Lavin, Tonia Rock,

Bly Straube, and Elizabeth Kostelny; and, of course, Bill Kelso, whose

dedication to Historic Jamestowne is an inspiration to all.

CONTENTS

FOREWORD

The short stories in this book are about the early years of the Jamestown Colony. The characters are real people who came to the first English settlement in the New World. Each story is about a real artifact uncovered by the Jamestown Rediscovery archaeologists from the site of the James Fort built in 1607.

The stories themselves are fictional but could possibly have happened. Many true historical facts are included in these stories. These facts come from maps, journals, letters, etc., taken from a series of books, JAMESTOWN REDISCOVERY I – VII, published by the Association for the Preservation of Virginia Antiquities (APVA). These books record the progress of the archaeological project now underway. They were the main source of information for the author. A few words may be unknown to you. They are underlined in the stories and defined in the Glossary.

The artifacts uncovered and the facts known are combined with some imagination to create interesting stories about life in Virginia some 400 years ago. While you enjoy the stories, you can learn a lot about life in colonial times.

To get ready to read, two short sections, "What is Archaeology?" and "About Jamestowne," are included.

Read these stories. Meet the brave colonists. Think about these interesting artifacts from the past. What stories do you believe they tell?

Jamestowne's Uncovered Treasures

WHAT IS
ARCHAEOLOGY?

Archaeology is scientific.

Archaeology is mysterious.

Archaeology is exciting.

Archaeology is challenging.

Archaeologists are like detectives; they have inquiring minds. They discover things in the ground that give us clues to the past. Archaeologists do scientific digging by laying out a measured grid system or squares. They must be very organized and neat, and they must record each "find" that they uncover. These "finds" are called <u>artifacts</u> and "footprints." Once objects are removed, and the ground is disturbed, the archaeologists must leave very careful records and photographs of *where* everything came from so that future generations can also learn about the past.

Finding the artifacts is only part of the process for the archaeologists; the artifacts must be treated carefully for ongoing studies. After artifacts are removed from the ground, they are washed, numbered, <u>catalogued</u> into a computer, photographed, and carefully stored in the laboratory. Metal and leather objects are treated with chemicals so that they are preserved before they decay or rust.

Archaeologists also do several types of scientific studies to learn about the people of the past. They use <u>ground radar surveys</u> to find possible disturbed areas in the soil, which indicate where people once lived. They do <u>carbon-dating</u> of burned objects to help discover how old the objects are. They study the bones of animals and seeds they find to see what people ate long ago. When human bones are found, archaeologists work with <u>forensic anthropologists</u> to learn whether the people were male, female, young, or old and whether they died from disease, from gunshot or arrow-point wounds, or simply from old age.

Archaeologists study records of those who lived long ago. Those working at Jamestown read journals of Captain John Smith, who became governor of Jamestown in 1608, and William Strachey, who was secretary of the colony in 1610. These records help them understand the past. Old maps are also studied. There is very little written material from this time period, which makes these "unknown" discoveries from the ground very valuable in providing information.

The archaeologists at Jamestown have a very important role in telling the story of how the people at Jamestown lived. They find "footprints" in the ground, which are often just soil stains from the wooden <u>palisade</u> posts, buildings, cellars, ditches, moats, and wells — all parts of the fort built in 1607. These are things that can no longer be seen above ground level.

Archaeologists also find objects, such as helmets, breastplates, gun parts, bottles, locks, sword hilts, cooking vessels, Indian arrowheads, and jewelry. It is exciting to discover these things from the past.

The stories that follow tell about several of the objects, or artifacts, found in the Jamestown Fort excavation. Only a few of the 500,000 objects already found are used to bring the early Jamestown settlement "back to life."

Ellen Kelso

ABOUT
JAMESTOWNE

The first 107 men and boys who arrived at Jamestown along with a crew of sailors left England in 1606 to sail to Virginia. They brought everything they possibly could with them to help start their new lives in the new colony in Virginia which was called Jamestown. They brought guns and helmets, cooking utensils, storage jars, books, pottery, jewelry, coins, and tools. The three small sailing ships — the Susan Constant, the Godspeed, and the Discovery — were crowded with their supplies, themselves, and even live animals such as chickens and pigs that they could eat when they arrived on the other side of the Atlantic Ocean. There was no way to keep things fresh, so the meats were salted to preserve them. They could not drink salty ocean water, so they had to bring fresh water in barrels, which took up lots of space. They brought vegetables that would last many weeks and lots of a very hard bread called "hardtack."

The colonists encountered many problems. They thought their voyage would take about three months, but the winds were not always blowing, and instead the trip took about four and a half months. Much of the food they had planned to bring to the new colony had to be eaten on board the ship before they ever reached land. When the settlers arrived on May 13, 1607, the spring growing season was nearly over. During the first seven years there was a drought, which meant there was very little rain to help grow crops. Lack of food was a problem! The men hunted for deer, squirrels, rabbits, raccoons, and fox. They fished in the James River for turtles and very large fish called <u>sturgeon</u>. They also got crabs, oysters, and clams from the river. The colonists got so hungry during the period called the "Starving Time" in 1609 and 1610 that they ate even snakes and mice, and finally their own dogs and horses. Lack of food was not their only challenge. The early settlers who left England in 1606 in search of silver and gold did not find these things at Jamestown. Instead they found an island that had no fresh water springs, so they were forced to drink from the salty James River, which made them sick. The mosquitoes caused diseases; the serious shortage of rainfall for growing crops caused hunger; and the hot, humid summers and very cold winters were quite unlike their homeland of England.

Danger was always a threat. They chose the island to settle on, so they could protect themselves from the Spanish war ships and the Indians, who sometimes would attack them. But many times the Indians were their friends. In the beginning, the Indians would bring them fresh vegetables, such as corn, squash, and pumpkins. As time went on, the colonists would barter or trade for food. The Indians were very interested in trinkets and objects that were shiny or noisy, such as decorative beads or copper pieces made into necklaces by the colonists.

Because the settlers had so little room on their ships to bring many pots and pans, as well as other things, the archaeologists found many items that had been recycled. An example is a breastplate used as armor in battle made into a cooking pot. Turning one thing into another was quite common, because there were no stores where they could go to buy new things. They had to wait for a supply ship to come from England, which could take many months or even a year.

Jamestown remained the capitol of Virginia for ninety-two years. In 1699, the capitol was moved to what is now Williamsburg, Virginia. However, people have continued to live on Jamestown Island even up to the present time. That is why it is called the first **permanent** English settlement. We are thankful for these brave men and women who came in search of a new life that was better than what they had in England.

The work at Jamestown is especially important to our country for many reasons:

- Jamestown was settled by the English in 1607 and became the first **permanent** English colony in North America.
- The House of Burgesses first met in 1619 at Jamestown, which was the beginning of representative government in our country. This is the form of government we have today, where people vote to decide who our leaders will be and what laws we follow.
- English has always been the national language of our country.
- Trade with other countries began with Jamestown. Many goods, such as lumber, and tobacco, brought income to the colony.

Ellen Kelso

JAMIE'S PET:
FRIEND OR FOOD?

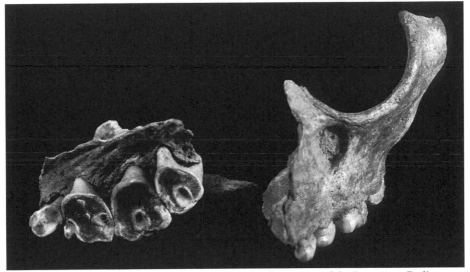

This raccoon jawbone was uncovered very early in the first season of the Jamestown Rediscovery project (1994). On close examination, archaeologists determined the teeth were quite worn down, indicating that the animal was old before dying and may have been a pet.

Jamestown Rediscovery I, 1995
Association for the Preservation of Virginia Antiquities

The summer sun of 1608 beat down on the clay floor of the <u>forge</u> at the fort on Jamestown Island. The tall <u>palisade</u> walls, made of tree trunks, protected the early settlers, but also kept out any bit of breeze from the nearby James River. Young James "Jamie" Brumfield's arms and shoulders ached after hours of pumping the <u>bellows</u> for Richard Dole, a blacksmith. Richard was a big man, always hungry and looking for something extra to eat. He often teased Jamie about being a "little lad" with no need for much food. You see, food was of great importance to all those at Jamestown. Richard was repairing a musket for a colonist soon to be posted on guard duty on a <u>bulwark</u> of the fort. He dare not report for duty unarmed, because the threat of attack by the Indians, the "naturals," was very real.

Every person had work to do at Jamestown. When Jamie was not helping the blacksmith, he was busy with other craftsmen. He might grind glass in a small cup, called a <u>crucible</u>; this was one step in making glass. At other times, he might smooth the surface of a clay jar before the craftsman baked it. Clay objects were used in many ways for eating, drinking, and storing things. Jamie was too young for all the exciting chores like hunting deer and turkeys or fishing for <u>sturgeon</u>. He looked forward to the day he would be allowed to go alone outside the wooden walls of the fort.

After Richard closed the forge for the night, Jamie, with sagging shoulders and sooty face, walked the short distance home to the <u>longhouse</u> where he lived with other men and boys. It was crowded and smelled of dirty sweat after a long work day. Supper, prepared over an open fire, consisted of fish and corn, sometimes rabbit or deer.

With darkness came sleep — rest for another busy day. After work Jamie always chose to stay outside until bedtime to play with Snooker, his pet raccoon. Finding the little pet was quite an interesting incident.

Only days after the arrival at Jamestown, everyone helped build the wooden fort for protection. Jamie and two older colonists were out in the woods chopping trees and dragging them to the fort site. One day they discovered a large hollow log and heard unusual noises from inside. The men tipped the log, and a most interesting animal tumbled out. Small and furry, the creature had a long tail with black rings and black around its eyes. At first he was frightened, but Jamie spoke to him and, with bread from his pocket, lured him to follow as the team returned to the settlement. As time passed, he and Jamie became good friends, and now the raccoon lived inside the fort.

Under some heavy brush a safe distance from the longhouse, Jamie kept Snooker in a cage. It was made of strong sticks bound together with reeds from the river. Food was hard to come by at Jamestown now, but Jamie saved bits of his own supper to feed his friend. Snooker, with his amazing front paws, took the food gently, cleaned it, and ate it bit by bit. Jamie enjoyed watching the process. Snooker's ringed tail and masked face were not found on furry creatures in England. He was a special friend, for there were few boys Jamie's age in the settlement, and even so, there was little time for play.

Both boy and raccoon seemed content at the new Jamestown colony for the first few weeks, until the hot, humid summer days arrived. Many colonists became too sick to work, to hunt, or to fish. Their energy was spent burying those who did not survive the hard times. Everyone was hungry. Jamie sometimes noticed the hungry men looking greedily at the little animal whose skinned and roasted body would provide some small meal for a few settlers. Richard, the blacksmith, was especially hungry. He would laugh and tease Jamie, telling him to throw the raccoon on the fire and serve his fellowmen a tasty treat. Jamie kept a watchful eye on his pet, hiding his cage carefully, moving it from place to place. Always he made certain it was covered with brush and tree branches.

At night by the firelight, healthier men spoke of returning to England, giving up this hopeless idea of a colony in the New World. Things were certainly not as they expected. Jamie, with Snooker by his side, listened as

3

the future of Jamestown was debated. The boy was fearful, but hopeful, for his new home.

As the hot summer continued, living conditions did not improve. More men became ill and more died. They desperately needed food and good water. Richard's teasing continued. Jamie realized the situation was serious. What should he do? Many questions came to mind: Should I sacrifice my pet, my good friend, for the small amount of food he would provide? Would Snooker have a better life outside the fort? Were his brothers and sisters there? What was life like beyond the palisade walls? Did Indian boys have pets to play with and chores to do? At last Jamie had a plan to save Snooker. He knew, as a young English boy, he could not survive beyond the palisade walls, but Snooker could!

A bright, full moon was shining the night Jamie slipped from his pallet on the floor of the longhouse. He crept past the snoring sleepers to the quiet outside. Only smoke remained from the evening fire. He found Snooker's cage hidden in the thick brush. He unfastened the reeds and gently cradled his furry friend in his arms. Earlier that day Jamie had dug a small opening under the nearby palisade — enough room for a small raccoon to escape to freedom and the familiar surroundings that lay beyond the small world within the fort.

Parting with Snooker was more difficult than Jamie expected, but there was really no choice. He must escape the starving colonists, and this seemed the only way. Jamie stroked Snooker's soft fur and hugged him one last time. Then he removed from his pocket a large bite of roasted rabbit and let the raccoon get a good whiff of it. He placed the meat on a leaf near the opening. With a long stick he pushed the food as far as he could to the other side of the wall. Gently Jamie pushed Snooker through the hole toward the waiting bit of food. Once he was beyond the palisade wall, Jamie quickly filled the hole, packed the soil securely and placed a log across the spot to make sure of the closure.

Jamie sat quietly for several minutes hoping to hear some sounds to indicate that Snooker was safe on the other side. Silence filled the night. Jamie slowly, sadly made his way back to his straw pallet. He fell asleep thinking of Snooker playing safely in the forest. Tomorrow he would be back to work and back to his unknown future as a young boy of early Jamestown.

BURGLARY AT
THE BULWARK

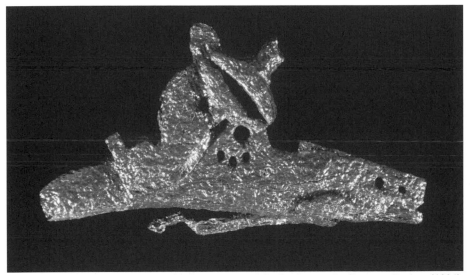

This pistol was uncovered during the first season of the Jamestown Rediscovery Project (1994). This Scottish pistol dates "to the late 16th century and probably belonged to one of Jamestown's gentlemen."

Jamestown Rediscovery IV, 1998
Association for the Preservation of Virginia Antiquities

   Cold clouds of damp mist hung over the wooden <u>palisade</u> walls of the Jamestown fort. The night was ghostly quiet as armed guards posted on the <u>bulwarks</u> paced slowly, peering into the darkness. Back and forth, back and forth, they kept watch over the sleeping fort.

   Stephen, the guard nearest the river, stopped to pack his clay pipe. Indian tobacco was bitter, but smoking would keep him awake. It was hoped that the tobacco plants John Rolfe got from the West Indies would mix well with the Indian leaf and improve the flavor. Who knew? It was an experiment for the new Virginia colony. Perhaps it would prove to be a successful one.

As Stephen brought a flame to the small bowl of the long, slim, clay pipe, he heard an unusual sound from the river — a scrape on the beach. Had a log washed ashore? There was the sound again. Stephen whistled to signal his fellow guards. His call was answered by movement in the darkness. Were these rustling sounds coming from the fort or from the river? Stephen listened as running footsteps came closer — whose footsteps?

Suddenly strong bare arms surrounded Stephen's chest. He was unable to move. Without question, the Indian intruder was not alone; a second one grabbed his pistol from his belt. He threw the weapon over the palisade wall! Was someone outside waiting? Almost in the same moment, the other guards, having heard the whistle, rushed to rescue their fellow colonist and capture the Indians.

Within minutes the noise from the bulwark brought others running to support the guards. The two Indians were captured. A small party of colonists with flaming, wooden torches searched the ground outside the fort for the stolen weapon, but the pistol was nowhere to be found. The prisoners were bound and locked in the cellar of the <u>blockhouse</u>. For the moment, peace was restored.

The long, narrow blockhouse supported the eastern wall of the fort. Supplies of all types were stored there: food, tools, weapons. This building had a deep cellar with walls and floors, even steps of hard clay. Jamestown clay made it difficult to plant crops needed for food, but it was well-suited for other things like making pottery and bricks. Because the blockhouse held supplies, it was guarded at all times. Colonists desperate for food often tried to break into the storeroom. Life was hard in early Jamestown. An Indian attack such as this made the settlers more fearful.

What would become of the prisoners? It was found that they were, in fact, brothers. John Smith, the President of the colony, wanted to keep peace with the natives, but stealing weapons could not be overlooked. Every gun and pistol was necessary to protect the struggling settlers. Safety and survival of the colony were still uncertain.

Bound hand and foot, the two Indians were confused and frightened as they sat in the dark, damp cellar. They sang strange chants in their native language and swayed from side to side preparing for what was to happen next.

Morning brought another search for the missing pistol. It was not found. As Stephen suspected, a third Indian must have been outside the wall to take the gun. The Indians wanted the power of the "fire-sticks," and they would risk a great deal to get this power.

Guards came to the cellar of the blockhouse to take the prisoners outside to stand before the <u>Council</u> and its leader, Captain John Smith. Tossing their heads of long black hair and glancing with wild, shiny eyes from one colonist to another, they were dragged to the clearing where the Council waited. These men sat with stern faces turned toward the Indian brothers. Their crime was not a small matter. Weapons, like food and tools, were needed for survival.

After some discussion, John Smith made a deal with the brothers. He would release one of them to find the pistol and return it by sundown. When the weapon was returned, the two would be set free. Meanwhile, one Indian prisoner was to remain in the cold, windowless cellar. The two seemed to understand Smith's terms. One agreed to stay; the other, to find the pistol and return it.

After several hours Smith sent food and some charcoal for a fire to the Indian who remained in the blockhouse. Toward evening the second Indian returned with the stolen pistol. A guard was sent to get the

prisoner. He was found unconscious — smothered from the smoke of the fire in the closed cellar. The colonists believed him to be dead.

John Smith then made a second deal with the Indian who had returned the pistol. If, after this, they would only come to the fort in peace, he would bring his brother back to life. A very strong drink was given to the prisoner and he was revived. The Indian brothers soon went away and told their fellow tribesmen that Captain John Smith could "bring back the dead."

TRINKETS
FOR TRADE

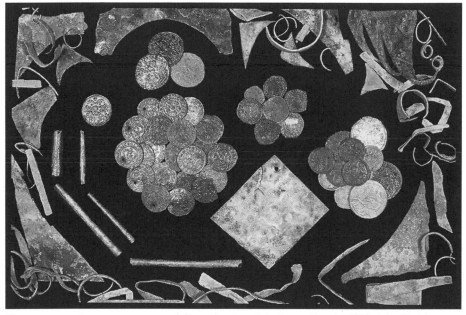

These copper pieces were recovered from the site of the James Fort in 1999. John Smith wrote that objects like these were invaluable for trade with the Powhatan Indians.

Jamestown Rediscovery V, 1999
Association for the Preservation of Virginia Antiquities

"Aye, captain, you sent for me?" asked Samuel Collier as he entered the tent. John Smith looked up from cleaning his <u>matchlock</u> gun.

"Yes, lad, come and sit. Let's talk a bit. The time seems right for getting to know our Indian neighbors a bit better. For the most part they are friendly and at times have brought us food. However, we need more understanding of their ways. Do you not agree?"

"Indeed, sir, but how do you plan to learn more about them? Our earlier exploration along the river with Captain Newport brought both friendly meetings and hostile attacks. Their ways are confusing. We cannot even speak their language. A few gestures help, but — "

"Exactly." Smith broke in. "Now here is my plan. I would like you to go as my scout and live among the <u>Powhatans</u> for a time. Learn their language and, I might add, their ways of fighting, in the event we may need such information in the future."

Samuel Collier was about twelve years of age. He had left his home and family in Lincolnshire, England, with dreams of adventure in the New World. He joined the first colonists as the page of Captain John Smith. Now in this new colony of Jamestown John Smith had become the leader of the small band of men and boys. Samuel Collier was his trusted and devoted servant.

First and foremost a soldier, Smith made sure the colonists followed his military rules. He believed if the colony was to survive, everyone must be required to work. "If you do not work, you do not eat" was Smith's motto. Even though harsh, his leadership helped to establish and strengthen the colony.

Another of John Smith's major concerns was to keep peace with the Indians living nearby. How was this to be done? The colonists knew nothing about Indian culture or language. Smith's plan to send young Samuel Collier to live with them was clever, but also dangerous.

"Captain, sir," responded Samuel, "you know I do as you command. My skills are not in language or warfare. You have taught me much about defending myself, and for that I am most grateful. I will go try to learn more about Chief Powhatan's people."

"Your devotion to our cause and to me is honorable, Samuel. Skills in language are important, but your ability to defend yourself in case of trouble is even more important," said Smith.

Only a few days later Smith received word that Powhatan agreed to his plan. Samuel Collier traveled alone and unarmed to an Indian settlement a few miles from Jamestown. He carried with him several small knives, some shiny bells, and a small axe to offer in trade. He was without a proper map; he had only a pocket compass to guide him.

Samuel traveled off his course into some unknown areas of the island. He saw smoke from a campfire nearby and heard Indian voices. Samuel knew these were not coming from the village he was to visit. Who were these Indians? Were they friendly? As he came closer to their campfire, he saw they were a hunting party preparing their weapons. Samuel walked bravely into their circle with his hand over his heart in a friendly greeting. They watched him in silence. Samuel showed them that he carried no weapon. The leader of the group, who wore more feathers than the others, stood and walked toward their visitor.

Samuel's heart pounded in his chest. How could he show that he came in peace? As he stepped back, his hand touched his small compass. "Look at this," Samuel called, "It shows the way through the woods!" The Indian stopped and looked at the object. Samuel held the compass, changing directions and showing the bouncing needle. The leader was curious, thinking this was a magic object. The speech of these natives did not sound angry. Samuel was relieved. He took from his coat one of the small knives and offered it to the Indian leader.

With gestures and drawings in the dirt, the Indians began to understand that Samuel — sent by John Smith, whom they knew — was going to their village. They gave him a few directions and he was, once again, on his way. He could feel his heart pounding as he walked away. He was afraid but also very proud of his first meeting with the natives of the new land.

. . . .

Several months later Samuel returned to Jamestown wearing deerskin clothing and carrying a long bow of ash wood. He returned with his own plan for keeping peace with the Indians and helping the struggling colony. Meeting with John Smith, he declared, "We cannot deal with these natives in peace or in war as before. The soldiers among us must learn new ways of fighting."

"Then, my 'Indian friend', for you have the look of a Powhatan brave, what do you suggest?" asked Smith.

"I have no ready answer, sir," said Samuel, "but consider this problem for future discussion with the Council. Our fellowmen must be prepared for fighting the Indians when necessary. There is other important information to share."

"Speak of it, I pray you," urged John Smith.

"We know our native neighbors place much value in small, shiny trinkets to own and to wear. They attach all such items, as well as animal bones and teeth, to their deerskin clothing. They believe such decorations keep them from harm. We must find and make such items to satisfy their desire for them. Then we may find them more friendly and get even more food from them. It seems we should inform our fellow colonists of this custom. Our comrades may own small trinkets even now to trade. Then, may we not engage our craftsmen to make such items? Our native friends are to be dealt with. Let us find peaceful ways, lest we go to war with them."

"Samuel, you have learned much, and your ideas are worth consideration. Trading with our neighbors to keep them at peace is certainly something which must be encouraged," responded Smith.

"Oh, yes, another thing," continued Collier, "one special prize for these natives is copper metal, of any size, to adorn their bodies. They believe it to be most valuable in protecting them from 'evil spirits.' Have

I not seen several items of copper among our supplies? A drinking cup? A teapot? May we ask, or require, that the owners give these copper objects to be cut into small pieces to use to please our Indian friends? Trust my word, sir, they place much value in copper of any size or shape."

"Samuel, I do recall seeing a small, simple piece of copper hanging around the neck of a Powhatan chief. Your idea is an excellent one! I will indeed give much thought to your plan and share your report with the Council at our next meeting."

Placing his strong hand on Samuel's shoulder, John Smith spoke sincerely, "My good and loyal young friend, you have done well, and I have only the highest regard for you. Jamestown is indeed fortunate to have you among its company!"

THE BLUE BEADS

During the first year of the Jamestown Rediscovery project seventy beads were uncovered. Beads like these were very valuable in trading with the Indians – especially those of sky-blue color.

Jamestown Rediscovery I, 1995
Association for the Preservation of Virginia Antiquities

"Hear ye! Hear ye!" called the secretary of the Council. The Jamestown settlers gathered near the church every Monday morning to learn of their work assignments for the week and to hear news from their leaders. Everyone hoped to hear that a supply ship arrived, but the settlers dreaded the news that another of their small group may have died. Now only a few of them were able-bodied enough to continue the hard work of building the new colony. There were still <u>palisade</u> walls to build, deer and turkeys to shoot, fish to catch, and crops to plant. There was much to do.

Thirty or so rather ragged-looking men and boys stood together. Some sat leaning against trees; others, down on one knee. All looked dirty and discouraged. Many murmured about the difficult duties that were assigned.

"There's too much work for too few men," said one. "Do all the 'gentlemen' work as hard we us commoners do?" asked another man. "My home back in England seems better every day," said a third.

After the duties were divided among the group, Council President John Smith raised his hand and called for quiet. Everyone listened when Captain Smith spoke. He was a strong and able leader, but a very strict one. "Some days ago, my young page Samuel Collier returned, as you know, from a time with one of Chief Powhatan's Indian tribes," announced Smith. "He learned a number of interesting and helpful things from his stay with them — all of which will be shared with you as time permits and need directs."

"All we want to know is how to protect ourselves from their arrows and tomahawks," said one sour-faced settler.

"I'd say so as well," responded the friend standing beside him.

"My comrades," continued Smith, "there is much to learn of the Indian customs, as well as how they fight. If our colony is to survive, we must try to keep peace with these natives. Remember they far outnumber us. They know this island well. We have much to learn from them."

The colonists listened as John Smith spoke further. "Samuel reports what I have already experienced in my travels. Trade with these natives will prove most important until our own crops are harvested and we have learned to hunt and fish successfully. Until we are established, we need their friendship and help.

"Concerning items for trading, young Collier brings news of the Indians' desire to own all kinds of shiny trinkets to attach to their clothing. They also have a fondness for beads, especially those of sky-blue color. I recall that several of you carry beads of this type. Perhaps they are tokens from your wives or sweethearts back in England. What better way to honor those loved ones than by trading these lovely beads for our own health and safety?

"Also," continued Smith, "among all things, these Indian neighbors of ours believe copper pieces worn as jewelry are most valuable to keep away evil spirits.

"The Council requires that, if you have such items among your personal belongings, you deliver them to the Reverend Robert Hunt to be used by those who work outside the walls of the fort. They will not be used to trade unless the need arises. Reverend Hunt will keep a record of your contributions."

Walking away, several settlers spoke frankly. "High time, I'd say, to require our gentlemen to give more," said one. "They do very little of the hard work, knowing nothing about it. They surely can give of their valued possessions," said another. "They own, most certainly, the items described by Captain Smith. We have little of that to offer."

During the following several days, Reverend Hunt sat near a table in front of the church to collect the items for trade. A few copper pots were presented. Tin bells and metal tokens were collected. Several beads were also contributed. These were perhaps the most valuable of all. Reverend Hunt thanked those who gave and recorded each item and its owner.

It happened that on one such day Pocahontas, favorite daughter of Chief Powhatan, came to the fort bringing corn and a wild turkey. She came with one of her brothers, Pochins. During the months of peace with the Indians, she often came with food for the hungry settlers.

This was the first visit by Pochins to the fort of the Englishmen. He was quite curious about these new, fair-haired people who wore such unusual clothing. He walked among the laborers, watching them work with tools that he had never seen before. He watched the blacksmith working over the heat of the <u>forge</u> fire. He visited the church and saw the table spread with trade items. Never had he seen such beautiful things! He reached to touch them. Reverend Hunt tried, in a kind way, to explain the meaning of the collection.

"These, my young friend, are owned by the men here. They are allowing our leaders to keep them and use them for trade with your people," explained Reverend Hunt.

Pochins' eyes fell on three blue beads on a deer-hide string. His look was one of desire. He pointed to the beads and to himself. There was no question about his message. He wanted the blue beads! John Smith observed the scene. What should be done? Here is the son of Chief Powhatan. He comes with Pocahontas to bring food. How can we refuse him?

John Smith picked up other items on the table to show the young boy as substitutes for the valuable beads. Pochins shook his head and, once again, pointed to the beads and then to himself.

"Perhaps it is best," thought Smith, "to give the beads to him. He will return to Powhatan and show him that the English settlers have valuable things to trade for food and for their friendship."

Once the beads were in his possession, Pochins hugged John Smith and Reverend Hunt. He jumped and yelled with delight. He ran to find his sister to tell her of his good fortune and show her the beautiful blue beads.

Pocahontas came to the church. She turned to John Smith with a questioning look. Smith then helped her understand that he did, indeed, give the beads to Pochins. His message to her and to her brother was one of thankfulness for their gifts of food. It was also a sign of friendship to the Indians of Chief Powhatan's tribes.

THE PIKE-HEAD SPEAR

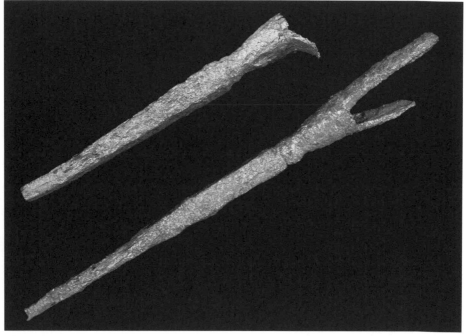

These iron heads of two spikes were uncovered in 1998 from Pit 1 of the Jamestown Rediscovery archaeological site.

Jamestown Rediscovery IV, 1998
Association for the Preservation of Virginia Antiquities

Young Richard Mutton walked slowly along the edge of the James River. The toes of his bare feet sank into the sandy mud. The water was cool, helping to reduce the hot, humid summer air of Jamestown. Richard walked outside the <u>palisade</u> walls with Mr. Keale, the <u>fishmonger</u>, who needed to repair a net for catching the large fish called <u>sturgeon</u>. These fish were a main source of food for the Jamestown settlers.

Richard liked being near the water. His home in London was near the <u>Thames River</u>. Often with <u>Mum,</u> he would walk down, take off his shoes and socks, and wade in the cool water, just as he was this day at Jamestown. How Richard missed his home and family! Life at Jamestown was filled with adventure — seeing new things, learning new skills — but it was also a hard life. There was much work to do and sometimes little to eat.

"Don't wander too far away, lad," called Mr. Keale. "I'll soon be done here and ready to get back inside the fort."

"Yes sir, Mr. Keale, I'll stay nearby," called Richard. As he spoke, his foot struck an object in the mud. "What's this?" he said to himself. Reaching down, Richard picked up a metal object, quite sharp on one end and open on the other — a long, pointed cone. He washed it in the river water and ran to show it to his friend. "Mr. Keale, sir, what might this strange object be?" he asked excitedly.

"Well, let me have a look now," said Mr. Keale. "You may have found a treasure!" Taking it from Richard, Mr. Keale examined it carefully. "Why, I believe this is a <u>pike head</u>. I'm no soldier, but I've seen such as this before."

"What would a soldier be using this for?" Richard asked, somewhat puzzled.

"Well, a metal piece like this would be attached to a rather long staff or pole and used somewhat like a spear in fighting an enemy."

"Would such be used to fight Chief Powhatan's Indians?" asked Richard.

"I think not. Perhaps that is why this piece was tossed into the river. The pike is of little use fighting among the trees of the forest here on the island. Pikes were important weapons of warfare in Europe. My guess is they were brought here to fight the Spanish, if need be. We have the Indians, our enemies on land, and perhaps the Spanish on the sea," explained Mr. Keale.

"I'll keep this pike head," said Richard, drying it on his shirt. "I may someday need such a weapon as you describe."

"I hope not, my young friend, I do hope not."

The two returned to the fort. Once behind the safe palisade walls, Richard showed his treasure from the river to his young friends and explained its use just as Mr. Keale related it to him. Later at the campfire, it was passed around for others to see. "Yes, no doubt it is a pike head," said one colonist, an old soldier. "There is really little use for pikes here in Jamestown. Maybe another use could be found for such as this."

Lying on his straw <u>pallet</u> later that night, Richard examined the metal pike head. "Now, just how could this be used?" he thought. "We are always trying to make good use of everything." Richard fell asleep still holding the pike head in his hand.

Bright and early the next morning Richard ran in search of his friend, the fishmonger. Finding him among his fishing nets, Richard spoke, "Mr. Keale, sir, could my pike head perhaps be attached, as you explained, to the long narrow branch of a tree and be used to spear those fish we see near the shore? Could I help you fish with such a spear?" Richard asked.

"Why, what a clever boy you are!" responded Mr. Keale. "It is indeed worth a try."

After Richard's duties were done for the day, he searched for a strong, slim tree branch to trim for the shaft of his spear. "It must be of just the right size to fit securely on the metal pike head. It must also be heavy enough to withstand spearing a large fish," thought Richard.

What an exciting project! Every spare moment Richard worked on the spear. On occasion he imagined himself a soldier fighting the Spanish with the pike in position to attack.

At last the spear was ready to test. Mr. Keale and two others were ready to go fishing, and Richard had asked to go along, spear in hand, or "at the ready," as his father would say.

The day was hot, but the water was cool as Richard stepped in the river up to his knees. He moved slowly so he did not disturb his intended victims — the fish of the river. The sun cast a bright light on the water. Sometimes it helped him see the fish.

"There's a ripple on the water. Perhaps it is a large sturgeon," thought Richard. "No luck again. These slippery sea creatures are getting away from me. I expect they fear my weapon. They must see its shadow from the sunlight."

Richard tried again and again. He'd see a fish, aim, then throw his spear into the water, and the fish would swim away. What a disappointment! Back at the fort his friends were sure to tease him.

The fishing party was soon ready to return to the fort with a small net filled in part with fish. This would be food for supper cooked on racks above an open fire. The day's catch would be shared with everyone.

Head down, Richard walked beside Mr. Keale. "No luck today, my friend, with your new fishing pole?" he said. "Don't be discouraged. This happens often to me too. A fishmonger's work is many times unsuccessful. May I make a suggestion?"

"Oh please, sir." Richard said with a bit more interest. "I'd like your help."

"Next time, take some small pieces of bread, perhaps even some corn along," suggested Mr. Keale. "Tempt them with food. This may keep the fish near you, giving you a better chance to spear them. It may not work, but again, it is worth a try."

Several days later Mr. Keale and Richard were off to fish again. This time Richard packed bread crumbs into his pockets. His pike-head spear was in his hand. He felt like today he might spear a fish for his very own supper!

Richard stepped into the river with confidence. "Today surely the fish will come, and my new 'fishing pole' will move swiftly in my hand and spear a fish or two," he thought. He tossed a few bread crumbs into the water near him. He stood still and waited. Some crumbs drifted under the dark water; others floated on top. Sure enough, moments later, a rather large sturgeon swam near the surface to feed on the bread. Richard waited quietly. Just at the moment the fish opened his mouth,

Richard struck with his pike-head spear. The fish was caught on its sharp point. Richard pulled him from the river — the spear held high above his head with the struggling fish attached. His loud, long yell caused Mr. Keale and the other fishermen to stop and look for some wild Indian to jump at them from the trees. Instead they saw Richard, his spear, and his fish. They laughed and cheered his victory!

THE PUDDING POT

Men of James Fort made armor into more useful items, such as this breastplate made into a container or pot. It was recovered in 1999 at the fort site.

Jamestown Rediscovery V, 1999
Association for the Preservation of Virginia Antiquities

"Oh, Anne, I am so sick! The ocean is rolling, as is my stomach. Will we not soon arrive at Jamestown?"

"Mistress, the captain says we will be out of rough waters shortly and into the Chesapeake Bay. From there, we'll sail to the James River where our trip will be near its end."

The trip for Mistress Forest had been hard, for she was not at all well. Though only thirty-five years old, her body was filled with problems caused by her difficulty eating. Her teeth were bad, and many were gone; her eating was somewhat limited.

Mistress Forest, accompanied by her young maid-servant, Anne Burras, traveled to Jamestown to see her husband, Thomas, who came in 1607. This trip, know as the "second supply," arrived at the island in September of 1608. Mistress Forest and Anne Burras were probably the first English women to come to the new colony.

Thomas Forest, with the help of several other settlers, had prepared a small cabin for himself, his wife, and her servant away from the spying eyes of the others who lived in the longhouses. He gathered a few things that these ladies would need for housekeeping. There were pottery bowls and jugs, a cup or two, as well as several spoons and a knife. Homes in early Jamestown were quite different from those in England. Necessary items were in short supply.

"But, Thomas, how am I to cook for you? There is no cooking stove; there are no pots. I brought a few seasonings and powdered items with the clothes in my trunk, but if I have no way to cook, what will I do?"

"My dear," answered Thomas, "perhaps you can speak with our blacksmith, James Read. He may be able to help you."

James was a large, strong man with broad shoulders and a big job. As a blacksmith in early Jamestown, he was constantly called upon to repair iron objects, make tools and nails, and keep the military weapons in operation. He had a most important responsibility.

"Welcome to Virginia, Mistress Forest! It is a cheerful sight to see two womenfolk here. Now tell me, what is this your Thomas says you are in need of?"

"Mr. Read," began Mistress Forest, "as I see it, we must cook over an open fire. There seems to be no stove or oven to be used hereabouts. Cooking in this fashion requires some heavy pots. I wish to make some pudding for Thomas. I, myself, need such soft, sweet food, and I brought items from home to do just that. But, what am I to cook it in? Certainly a pottery bowl will not work. I need a heavy pot — a pudding pot. Do you think you can help me?"

Gazing into the <u>forge</u> fire for a long moment, James spoke. "Mistress Forest, of course I would like to help you and, better yet, I would like a small taste of that delicious pudding you are wishing to make. It has been a long while since the likes of that has crossed my lips. But a heavy cooking pot — I just do not know. Let me think on it. I'll let you know my answer soon enough."

September breezes from the river refreshed the Jamestown settlers. Perhaps the hot, humid summer was at last behind them. Even the bugs and other flying pests were gone. Anne Burras, the Forest's maid-servant, seemed to be happy on the island. She worked hard, as did everyone, but the prospect of a life in this new country was exciting. Surely other women and girls would follow with the next supply ship. Thomas Forest was indeed fortunate that his good wife, even in her weakened condition, was willing to bear the hardships of the sea journey to be with him during these difficult days as they established the new colony. He knew the conditions, over time, would improve, and the small band of settlers would grow. The colony would succeed in gaining a foothold in the New World.

Shortly after Mistress Forest visited him, James Read came knocking at the door of the Forest home.

"I believe," said James, "I have an answer for you, for the cooking pot you wish. Several weeks ago I found an armor breastplate, which had been discarded in the trench just outside the fort wall. Many such pieces have been discarded of late, as iron armor is of little value in fighting the Indians. Such protection is heavy and hot and causes our soldiers to move too slowly among the trees. Perhaps this breastplate can be heated and molded into your pudding pot!"

"Mr. Read, you are indeed a fine craftsman," said Mistress Forest. "Do try to do as you say. You and Thomas may soon have a fine pudding to eat!"

With much joy the blacksmith took to the task of creating the iron cooking pot for Mistress Forest. As he worked, he imagined sampling the tasty pudding. Back home in England, teas and meals quite often ended with such a treat.

Not long after his visit, James returned with the roughly-made pot. Only two days later Thomas Forest, James Read, and Anne Burras sat around a small wooden table as Mistress Forest served them a delicious English pudding.

THE GIFT

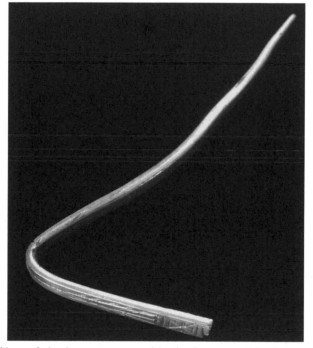

This silver bodkin, or hair pin, was uncovered in the first year of the Jamestown Rediscovery project. It came from the ditch near the fort wall.

Jamestown Rediscovery I, 1995
Association for the Preservation of Virginia Antiquities

Anne Burras wept quietly as she stood with Thomas Forest beside the grave of his dear wife. Mistress Forest was Anne's <u>patron,</u> who brought her, some months back, to the New World and Jamestown. The Reverend Robert Hunt now spoke of the courage of Mistress Forest as she withstood the long sea journey to be with Thomas, her beloved husband. Even though her health was poor, and life in the new colony was difficult, she risked all to be with him once again.

The coffin of yellow pine was lowered into the sandy clay of Jamestown as the small group watched silently. There had been so many such services, so many deaths among the colonists. Sometimes it seemed the settlement in the New World could not survive. Mistress Forest's determination gave them hope, which Reverend Hunt talked about in the funeral service.

The grave was placed within the <u>palisade</u> walls. Going outside for religious services was unwise. While the native Powhatan Indians had been friendly, for the most part, their beliefs and customs were unknown and feared by the colonists.

Following the arrival of Mistress Forest and Anne Burras, the first two women at Jamestown, others came with each new supply ship. The colony was indeed becoming a community. An enlarged fort with five palisade walls, instead of three, was constructed, with space for a few small homes for those who married. In many ways Jamestown was growing, but not without hardships as before. Food was scarce, the water was bad, and many died at an early age.

Anne Burras came to Jamestown as Mistress Forest's maid-servant. Her good husband, Thomas, would, no doubt, see to her well-being now that Mistress Forest was gone from them. He had said as much to Anne. She would cook and clean, do the housekeeping as before.

The mourners walked from the grave quietly. Anne and Thomas returned to their small home. They sat in silence drinking jugs of tea. Thomas spoke softly, "Anne, my good wife would want you to have her personal possessions, her clothing and such. You were not only her maid-servant but her very good friend. Without you she would never have traveled to Virginia to spend her remaining days with me. I am indeed thankful for this.

"Sir," replied Anne, "I thank you for the gift of my mistress' things. She was so very kind to me. She gave me this wonderful opportunity to come to the New World. I look forward to the future of our colony here. I wish to be a part of it."

Opening a small wooden box before him, Mr. Forest presented to Anne a small silver <u>bodkin</u> meant to be used to decorate a woman's hair. "This is perhaps the most valuable thing my wife owned, this silver bodkin. Please keep it to remember her and her kind nature. There is an effort now to collect such personal items to trade to the natives. I would be displeased to see that happen to this bodkin."

"Oh, sir, what a treasure indeed! I do thank you. I shall take the greatest care of this lovely piece. You are most generous!" As Anne spoke, tears of sadness and of thankfulness fell on her cheeks.

Some time following Mistress Forest's death, Anne was busy preparing herself for a very special evening. Since arriving at Jamestown, one colonist named John Laydon had paid her much attention. John often stopped his work to speak with her when they met. He was a laborer, and as such, he worked at many different tasks, from palisade construction to laying some of the first bricks made at Jamestown.

With permission from Mr. Forest, Anne planned to meet John one particular evening. They would perhaps walk by the river, then sit and talk about their lives back in England and their hopes for the future.

Preparing for this special evening was most exciting for Anne. Perhaps she would consider wearing a garment once belonging to Mistress Forest. It had been a proper amount of time since her death, and she knew Mr. Forest would approve. Mistress Forest brought two dresses with her from England. One was dark green, of a heavy fabric for cold weather. The other was blue in color, made of light linen. This blue one seemed better for the warm, humid night air of Jamestown Island. Both dresses were certainly better than anything Anne wore, but would they fit her? Quickly she slipped the blue one over her head. It fell from her shoulders into folds at her waist. Alas, it was too big, for Anne was only fourteen years old and very small. Could it possibly be fixed in time?

Hurriedly, she walked along the path to the <u>longhouse</u> where Thomas Hope, a tailor, often worked to repair and make clothing. Perhaps he would help her. Thomas Hope was one of those who traveled with Mistress Forest and Anne from England. He remembered her and put his hand to fixing the dress quickly.

Only a short time later Anne was back home with the blue linen dress tucked at the waist by Mr. Hope's nimble fingers. She must now clean her face and arms with a bit of Mistress Forest's lavender soap, then comb and style her long dark hair.

Anne looked into the hand mirror, which once belonged to Mistress Forest. She ran her fingers through her hair. The salty river water seemed to clean it, but once dried, her hair was dull and lifeless. She tried to collect fresh rain water to clean it, but there had been very little rain lately. The plants were dry and wilted, just like Anne's hair.

She twisted and pinned her hair into a loose fold on top of her head. If only she had a ribbon to add or a comb. "Oh, I know the very thing!" she said aloud, taking the small wooden box from her trunk. "The silver bodkin, the gift from Thomas!" Quickly she pushed it securely into the folds of her hair. Once again, she looked at her reflection in the window. Now she was ready for a special evening with young John Laydon!

· · · · · · · · · ·

Some months later, Anne Burras and John Laydon were wed by the Reverend Robert Hunt. They settled some miles from Jamestown. Their first child was a daughter and was named, most fittingly, "Virginia." She was the first child to be born in the new colony. Baby Virginia was another new beginning in the new colony.

THE BROKEN LOCK

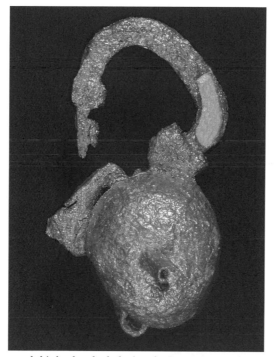

"Archaeologists uncovered this broken lock during the Jamestown Rediscovery excavation. It was found with a broken key inside – a key which does not fit the lock."

Association for the Preservation of Virginia Antiquities

The midnight sky was dark, with only a small sliver of the moon slipping out from among the clouds. The large figure of George Cassen peered around the corner of the <u>blockhouse</u>. Looking right, then left, he searched for the armed men assigned to guard this most important area of the fort. Inside the blockhouse was the storeroom where the food was kept — grain for making bread, corn for soup, fish and deer meat, maybe a rabbit or wild turkey. Food was precious in early

Jamestown. It was carefully divided among the settlers, with no one really given enough to satisfy his hunger.

George and his brother, Thomas, came to the new land after their mother and father died when their home near London, England, was destroyed by fire. These young men came looking for a new life, one filled with opportunity and promise. Their skills were limited, but their hopes were high. George was big and strong and somewhat slow to learn new things. Thomas was small, and life in the new colony was difficult for him. Even now he was back in the <u>longhouse</u> with a fever. George was worried about his brother, who was now his only family.

As George avoided the guards and slipped into the blockhouse, the humid night air filled his lungs as his rapid breathing showed the fear he felt. George must find food for Thomas; otherwise, his brother might die. Many of the colonists had already died from drinking the bad water and eating stale food. There was no way to keep the food from spoiling.

George had never been in the blockhouse. Only a few trusted men had the right to be near the food and guns that were stored there. He soon found a lighted torch hanging from the wall. Taking it, he moved slowly along the wooden walls searching for the storeroom door. He came upon some steps dug from the solid clay of the island. These steps led to a cellar. Perhaps the storeroom was down there.

Very few possessions were saved from the home of George and Thomas in England. The fire had destroyed the roof and walls, the furniture and clothes. Among the few objects they brought with them was the key to the door of their old home. George carried it in his pocket to remember his parents and his old life.

Now, as he moved down the steps to the cellar, he could barely see at one end a wooden door. It was closed and secured with a round lock. This must be the storeroom! As he leaned against the door, there was the faint scent of grain. This was the place he would find food for Thomas.

Bringing the torch closer, he examined the lock. He pulled, hoping to find it open, but this was not the case. Guards were always careful to keep the storeroom securely locked. How could he open the lock? By now George was filled with fear of being unable to get food for Thomas. Maybe, just maybe, the key in his pocket — the one he brought all the way from England — would unlock the storeroom door and make it possible for him to help his brother.

Noises from outside bothered George for a moment. His heart was beating wildly. Surely no one saw him come in. He had been so careful. It became quiet once again. He placed the torch against the clay wall and brought the old key from his pocket. It went into the lock! Maybe this would work. George's sweaty fingers slipped on the metal. Now, if the key would only turn. It was moving, but would it open the lock? Rubbing his hands on his pants to dry them, he was ready to try again. This time he turned the key as hard as he could. The key broke off in the lock and still it was unopened.

What was he to do? The key was stuck inside — evidence that someone had tampered with the storeroom lock! Someone tried to take supplies! George was searching for an answer. His toe hit a hard object on the cellar floor. Reaching down he discovered a large rock, probably used to prop the door open as supplies were moved. He took the heavy rock in one of his big hands. He pounded the lock with it until it was broken. Taking the torch once again, he went inside the storeroom. What would he find to take for Thomas to eat? What would make his brother well?

George found pieces of salted fish and some corn meal for mush. Quickly he filled his pockets. He then made his way up the steps and slipped quietly out of the blockhouse into the dark night. Only as he hurried back to the longhouse did George begin to realize what he had done and what trouble he was in with the other colonists and the Council that governed Jamestown. Would they not understand that he had to help his brother? They were not known to be kind and understanding. But he would worry about that later. Right now he needed to build a fire away from the longhouse to cook the fish and mush for Thomas. He hoped everyone would be asleep.

The long room was lined with sleeping, snoring men on straw <u>pallets</u>. Thomas sat, leaning against the wall. He was weak, but slowly he ate the food George offered. He was very tired; even chewing was hard for him. Thomas thanked George. Surely now he would begin to feel better and would soon be up and back to work. Completely exhausted, George lay down on his pallet near Thomas and fell into a deep sleep.

Early-morning light brought noisy activity inside the fort. In the longhouse, three armed men moved quickly alongside George's pallet. He awakened as angry faces looked down, and loud voices told him he was under arrest. Though weak, Thomas raised his head and called out, "Leave my brother alone! George did what he had to do to save my life!" The guards took no notice. They dragged George from his bed out into the bright sunlight. They took him to stand before the large wooden table where the Council members waited. Angry voices filled the air. Taking supplies was a most serious crime. With his eyes lowered and his shoulders slumped, George stood before the leaders. "Do you deny breaking into the storeroom? Taking food? You know the rules. The little food we have must be shared equally among all. What say you, George Cassen?"

The big man slowly lifted his head. His sad eyes met those of his accusers. He spoke softly and slowly. "Sirs, I did break the lock on the storeroom door. I went in and filled my pockets with corn and fish. The food was not for me but for my brother. Thomas is weak and sick with fever. He is the only member of my family yet alive. I cannot lose him. I have seen so many die from this same fever. Your Excellencies, he is all I have."

Low murmurs came from the group gathered to witness the hearing. Perhaps they were not so angry now, but somewhat sorrowful. Looking toward the longhouse, the colonists saw Thomas. He was painfully crawling toward the group. Grasping the low limbs of a small tree, he pulled himself to stand. The men stepped aside and became quiet so he could be seen and heard by the Council.

"Your Excellencies," Thomas began in a low, yet earnest, voice. "My brother did as you accuse him to save my life. As you know, George does not understand as most of us. He acts on ideas from his heart, rather than his head. I beg you gentlemen to forgive his shortcomings and free him. Let him continue his work building the shelters within our fort. He is strong and able to labor long hours for our new colony." Slumping down against the tree, Thomas ended his appeal.

The Council members withdrew into the church to reach a decision. George sat near Thomas, asking for a cup of fresh water for his brother. They waited as the sun shone warm on the small group within the Jamestown Fort.

As the Council returned to the table, George was brought to the front. All drew near to hear the decision. What would happen to George? The crime was serious, but the motive was understandable. Standing erect to address the group, John Smith, their proud and powerful leader, spoke.

"George Cassen has done wrong breaking into the storeroom and taking food not intended for him. This is a crime against all of us. His motive for this unlawful act was one of love for his brother, Thomas. It is the decision of this Council that the crime and the motive balance the scales of justice. We need George to live amongst us. He is a strong and willing worker. Let us require his promise that from this day forward he will obey all the laws of this colony, realizing that, when need is great, he should approach this Council for help."

"What say you, George Cassen? Will you so promise?" George answered in a strong, sincere voice, "I do, indeed, promise."

Captain Smith, addressing the entire group of colonists, said, "So be it, in the name of our sovereign King James I!"

ARROW-PROOF VESTS

A number of iron pieces with holes for attaching them to clothing were uncovered at the site of James Fort of 1607.

Jamestown Rediscovery V, 1999
Association for the Preservation of Virginia Antiquities

Streams of sweat fell from Robert Small's forehead, his armpits, his knees. The hot, humid air of Jamestown Island slowed the hunting party of men. Adding to the hot air, the men were ordered by their leader, Lord De la Warr, having recently arrived from England, to wear armor when outside the <u>palisade</u> walls of the fort. Iron breastplates and helmets were heavy and uncomfortable. The men could scarcely move to bring their <u>muskets</u> into firing position. They had fought earlier in the <u>Low Countries</u> of Europe. Armor was most important there. Breastplates protected them from lead shot, metal swords, and long, sharp <u>pikes</u>.

Combat with Indians in the Jamestown forest was altogether different. The enemy here was dressed in simple deerskin clothing and moved quickly, running from tree to tree, hiding behind small hills, jumping out from all sides with bow and arrow or tomahawk, ready to attack. The colonists had no time to ready themselves to fight. This was not war as they knew it, but short attacks meant to frighten the new settlers back into the fort, where the Indians hoped they would stay.

Before arriving at Jamestown, Robert Small had been a respected soldier. His skills in battle were well known. His leader, Lord De la Warr, and other Council members looked to Robert to train the inexperienced men in ways of fighting to protect their struggling settlement. Many of their company were gentlemen and craftsmen, those who had never been active in fighting, never even owned a weapon of any kind. Robert soon realized his experience as a soldier lacked knowledge of this new kind of combat.

Most of the Indians near Jamestown were friendly. Some even came with baskets of corn and fish to trade with the colonists. Among those

who came in peace was an Indian youth, Keeo, who became Robert's friend. Beginning with gestures and facial expressions, they learned to communicate. Slowly Robert and Keeo exchanged a few words from each of their languages. They grew to understand each other.

From Keeo, Robert slowly learned the Indians' fighting ways. He saw that the need for iron armor should be replaced by practice in running quickly among the trees, always being ready to draw and fire a loaded gun to defend the fort and its settlers.

Discarded armor, breastplates, and helmets were lying in the Jamestown sand waiting to be put to other uses. Nothing at Jamestown could be wasted.

With advice from James Read, a blacksmith, Robert approached the Council with a new way to protect colonists while hunting and fighting. The heavy iron breastplates could be divided into small rectangular pieces of iron with holes for attaching them in rows across the front of a vest-like jacket. Robert had seen such in earlier combat in Europe. These metal pieces were known as "jacks", and sewn onto a vest, they seemed to work very well as protection. This construction would allow the men quicker movement among the trees and greater access to their weapons. These garments would also be much cooler and would still protect the chest from Indian arrow points.

Lord De la Warr had a stern look as he listened to Robert's request. "I would never allow our few brave men to leave the fort without proper protection," he said. He, as well as others with him, believed in the old ways of fighting, as they had done in Europe years earlier. After much discussion Council members agreed to the construction of one of these vests of iron pieces, "jacks." Demonstrations of its use would follow within the walls of the fort.

Robert Small, with the help of the blacksmith, James Read, and a tailor, William Ward, set to work making the vest for testing. After long hours of construction, it was ready to try.

The armored vest proved to be a success! Vests of jacks became the popular protection for the fighting men of Jamestown. This was yet another small improvement in the life of the first English colonists in the New World of Virginia.

38

THE EAR PICKER

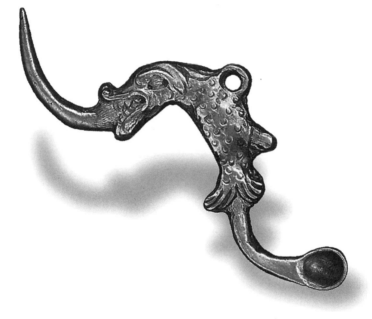

This ornate ear and tooth pick was found inside the fort extension.

Jamestown Rediscovery VII, 2001
Association for the Preservation of Virginia Antiquities

Edward Wingfield paced the deck of the Susan Constant swinging his watch chain, a proper gentleman from his hat with a feather to his fancy coat with shiny buttons. He took great strides across the deck. He was watching the ship's crew closely. He wanted to be certain they stayed busy.

He was not well liked by those traveling to the new land. Edward Wingfield seemed a rather self-centered man, and Nathaniel Peacock, his page, was somewhat fearful of him. However, the only way the young lad, Nathaniel, known as "Nate," could travel to the New World was in the service of a master. He was lucky to be selected by Master Wingfield to serve as his page.

The trip from England was long and hard. Once they arrived at the island, named by the colonists "Jamestown" for their king, there was much work to be done. The first task was to build a fort to protect them from the Indians and possibly the Spanish too. In just one month the wooden <u>palisade</u> walls were completed.

Master Edward Wingfield was a very important man. He was appointed the first president of the Jamestown colony. He acted very much like a king. He paced through the fort, always swinging his watch chain. Now and again a small silver object hanging from the chain caught the sunlight. Nate and his friends wondered what the trinket might be — a coin? a medal? a token?

"Your master seems unlike the others," Sam Collier remarked one day. "He strides along, looking down on everyone, swinging that chain of his. I am glad I am not his page. Nate, what do you know of this unusual piece he wears on his chain?"

Nate answered in an excited voice, "Well, almost every evening when he removes the chain, he places one end of the silver piece in his mouth. The other end he places first in one ear and then the other. It is a very strange habit!"

After listening to his two friends, Richard Mutton joined in, "Do you think the trinket is filled with strong spirits? But, if so, there would be no reason to put it in the ears. Perhaps it is medicine for all parts of the head."

"Nate, you must solve this mystery for all of us," ordered Sam. "Maybe after the good man retires and is asleep, you can get a closer look at his unusual object."

"Oh, lads," said Nate, "if Master Wingfield catches me looking about his things, I might be on the next ship bound for England, or I might be dead! Truth be known, I am most afraid of him."

Richard continued, "Nate, boy, you could surely think of a reason for examining Mr. Wingfield's things. Say, 'I'm shining your watch,' or 'I'm cleaning your buttons.' We all care for our masters' personal belongings. Please try it. We are wanting to know more about this strange object."

"Well, I'll do what I can. Now you two have got me wanting to know about this object myself," said Nate.

Sam joked, as he and Richard walked away, "Sweet dreams, dear sir, sweet dreams."

When supper was over, Nate hurried back to his <u>pallet</u> in the house of Edward Wingfield. Soon the captain came in. He took off his feathered hat, then his fancy coat. Next he removed the watch and chain, winding the watch for another day. He placed them on a stool near the foot of his bed. Then, he used the silver object as before. With one eye open, Nate watched carefully. There was very little light. The candle burned low. He needed to get close to the object, but how?

Once his master was snoring, Nate crept on hands and knees to the stool. Slowly he placed his chin on the top. He looked ever so closely at the watch. In the still darkness, its ticking sounded as loud as Big Ben in London. He saw very little, but he very carefully placed a hand on the chain and the small silver object. Ouch! One end of it was very sharp. This could be a small weapon. Feeling the other end, his finger found a very small bowl. Between the two was a rough part.

Wingfield turned over in his sleep, and Nate froze. "What am I doing?" he asked himself. "I'd better leave this for tonight and get to sleep."

Early the next morning, Sam and Richard pulled him aside. "Well, what happened last night?" asked Sam. "Did you try my plan when Wingfield was asleep?"

"Yes," Nate answered in an excited whisper. "I watched Master Wingfield take the watch and chain from his coat. Then, he put the silver object in his mouth and ears, just as before. Once he was sleeping soundly I crawled close to the object. It is most unusual — very sharp on one end, quite like a spike, and rounded on the other, as a very small bowl. The middle is different yet — very rough and hard to describe."

"What a mystery!" Richard said. "You have discovered a lot by feeling the thing. Do you think you could try to see the object now? Do you have your own candle, or could you get one?"

"This is no easy thing. How will a page like myself get a candle? And how will I keep it lighted after Master Wingfield goes to sleep?" asked Nate.

Always full of ideas, Sam said, "Tell Wingfield you want to read a while after going to bed."

"But I have no book to read," said Nate.

"What about writing a letter home?" asked Richard. "I can get some paper, pen, and ink from my master. He wants me to keep in touch with my family."

"Well, okay," said Nate, uncertain of the plan. "I guess I'll try to do it. You know, you lads could be leading me into a lot of trouble."

"How else can we find out about this unusual trinket?" asked Sam. "This has been a most interesting mystery. All due to you, Nate, boy."

Several nights later at bedtime, Nate, with writing materials in hand, went to Edward Wingfield. "Sir," Nate began, "might I have the use of a candle tonight to write a letter to my family back home? My friend, Richard, has given me paper and such. I'd like to write and tell them what a fine master you are and what an interesting experience these last months have been for me."

"Well, Nathaniel, you know candles are in short supply," said Wingfield. "But since you have not asked for special favors before, this one is permitted. Just see to it that you burn the candle for only long enough to write your letter. 'A fine master' you say — well now."

"Thank you, sir," replied Nate. "Thank you very much."

Following the evening meal of corn and smoked fish, Nate went to the wooden box and took out a candle — not a long one, for he did not want to anger his master. Some time later, Wingfield went to bed and quickly to sleep, leaving Nate writing by candlelight. He must complete his short letter quickly to have more time to examine the jewelry.

Wingfield slept soundly as Nate moved slowly with the light. Holding the candle as close as he dared, Nate stared at the strange silver object. It did have one very sharp end, and the other was a very small round spoon. Joining the two was the likeness of some type of fish or sea creature carved into the silver. What an odd design! He didn't know what to make of it.

Nate was up early the next morning. Before he returned the writing things to Richard, he drew, as best he could, the mysterious object. Both Richard and Sam looked puzzled at the drawing. What could this thing be?

The three boys worked hard all day helping laborers and craftsmen. Nate was tired and ready for sleep when a very angry Edward Wingfield stormed into the house. Nate shook with fear.

"Nathaniel!" shouted his master, "I have lost the small silver toothpick and ear scoop, my ear picker, which I keep at all times hanging on my watch chain! Have you seen it? Get up, boy, and help me look for it!"

"A toothpick and ear scoop, sir?" Nate asked. "And silver you say? I have seen nothing of it except on your chain, but I will help you look for it!"

Both man and boy looked through the entire house until darkness drove them to bed. Their search would begin again with daylight. As Nate lay down, he thought, "Think of it — a toothpick and ear scoop. One end picks, the other scoops. I cannot believe the things that gentlemen value. And I can hardly wait until morning to tell Richard and Sam!"

A SAD DAY

Parts of at least twelve matchlock rifles have been uncovered. This lockplate with trigger was taken from a pit inside the James Fort.

Jamestown Rediscovery IV, 1998
Association for the Preservation of Virginia Antiquities

The small, sad group passed near where two boys stood together speaking in whispers. "What happened to Captain Smith? There on the <u>litter</u>, he looks to be in great pain. Where are they taking him?" asked James Brumfield, one of the young boys who came to Jamestown with the first colonists in May of 1607.

"My understanding is that he must return to England for proper treatment of a very bad injury," answered Nathaniel Peacock, called "Nate." "But, here comes Sam, Smith's page. Surely he can answer our questions. Say there, Sam, what happened to Captain Smith?"

"Aye, mates! Well, some days ago, he, along with several others, was exploring westward, out beyond the island," Sam began. "You know, he cannot rest until he has tramped over every inch of this land. He wants to draw maps of the James River and the land areas along the shore. He has taken many of these short trips to explore and chart our new colony."

Sam continued. "Well, he had his <u>matchlock</u> rifle ready to fire at an attacking Indian or a frightened deer. Neither appeared, but there was some movement in the trees, and he fired quickly. A spark from his matchlock fell on his clothing and set fire to the gunpowder stored in a bag at his waist. The others rushed to him and put out the fire, but his side was badly burned."

"What a pity," said James, "our rifles do not always protect us."

The matchlock rifle was the most common firearm used by the early colonists. It was a very long gun and hard to fire. A lighted matchcord or "match" was needed in order to keep the rifle ready to fire. Gunpowder, often carried in a soldier's clothing, was dangerous. A match or spark caused many serious accidents.

James continued, "So, Sam, what brings us to this time of watching as our good leader is carried away? Must he return home, as Nate has said?"

"As you know, our surgeon, William Wilkinson, has already used much of the medicine brought from England. So many of our group have been ill or injured. We have no proper treatment for the captain here," explained Sam. "Pocahontas heard of the accident and asked her father, Chief Powhatan, to send a native priest or 'medicine man' to help."

These medicine men played an important part in the lives of the Indians living near Jamestown. Many believed they drove out evil spirits. They brought good luck in warfare and a successful harvest of crops. Medicine men were believed to have magic powers — to bring rain or to take away an enemy's power. Curing the sick was also one of a medicine man's most important jobs. They used herbs and other plants to make medicines for treating the sick.

"And what of this medicine man? Did he come? What did he do?" asked James excitedly.

"I was in the tent, but I could not see everything," continued Sam. "The Indian was dressed in very colorful clothing with many feathers and shiny trinkets. He danced around the fire making scary shadows on the walls. He sang and chanted too!"

"Go on, Sam, what happened next?" asked Nate. He wanted to know more about these mysterious methods.

"Well," said Sam, "he placed a bowl of water beside Captain Smith. Again and again he put his hand into the water and sprayed it on his own chest. He then moved tomahawk-like rattles over the captain's body. "As he shook these, he danced around. You could hear seeds or bones making a funny sound. This sound and that of the trinkets on his clothing were strange indeed."

"What sort of medicine did this man place on the captain's wound?" asked James.

Sam answered, "That is the strangest thing of all. He put nothing on the body. He only danced and chanted and surrounded Captain Smith with the noise from his rattles.

"How could such as this heal him?" wondered Nate.

"It didn't," Sam said with disappointment. "The native medicine man continued his treatment for several hours. Surgeon Wilkinson thanked him and offered him a knife in payment as he left. Then Mr. Wilkerson examined Captain Smith. Afterward, he turned to the others in the tent and sadly shook his head. There seemed to be nothing more he could do.

"John Smith is truly a hard, demanding leader, but how shall we ever survive without him? He has been the strong force of our colony," said Sam, and the others agreed.

As the boys turned to watch, the sad group moved slowly toward the ship anchored nearby in the James River. They felt worried and confused. They were alone. All those present felt the same. John Smith had brought order to the first permanent English colony. Many disliked his strict rule and his demanding work duties. However, most knew that during these first months as they struggled to start the settlement, they needed his strong leadership to survive. The new colony faced so many problems. Now, to lose their leader was too much to bear. It was a sad day, indeed, for Jamestown.

Note: John Smith never returned to Virginia again, but Pocahontas, her husband John Rolfe, and their son did see him on their visit to England.

TWO GOOD FRIENDS

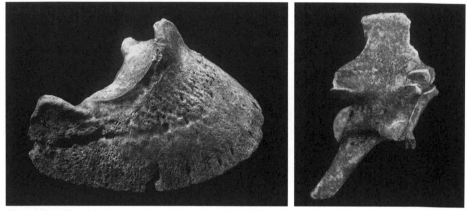

Horse's hoof and snake vertebrae from deposits of "food" remains.

Jamestown Rediscovery IV, 2000
Association for the Preservation of Virginia Antiquities

Richard Mutton was not certain of traveling to the new colony until Christopher Newport, captain of the expedition to the New World, allowed him to bring along his dog, Jack. There were only a few boys among the first settlers — four to be exact. They all became good friends, but, for Richard, his best friend was Jack.

Richard would never forget the trip from England. The small company left from Blackwall in December of 1606 and was delayed in the English Channel for several weeks, because the weather was bad for sailing. Once underway, their progress was slow. After a time in the Canary Islands, they sailed on to the West Indies. By May of 1607 they reached the Chesapeake Bay and the island now known as Jamestown. The ships were small and were crowded with more than a hundred hopeful colonists and a crew of sailors. One of the group died during the trip. Richard, and Jack as well, were glad to reach the solid ground of Jamestown Island. That was two years ago, and they had lots of hard work behind them. The new life of these first Virginians was teaching them a great deal.

The winter of 1609 was yet another hard time at Jamestown. In October, Captain John Smith returned to England. He was badly injured when gunpowder, stored in his pocket, caught fire and burned his upper leg. Captain Smith was not the most popular of leaders but was, by far, the most capable. Without strong leadership, the colonists could not survive.

Richard's master was George Kendall, one of the gentlemen of the colony. He obeyed as Master Kendall directed. Most days Richard helped the laborers. He worked long and hard with Jack by his side. When he became discouraged, Jack was always there to cheer him. They were two good friends.

Among the many hardships faced by the colonists during the winter of 1609 was the lack of food. The native Indians did not come to the island to trade their corn for knives and trinkets. The river, a source of good fishing, was frozen. The supply ships from England found it dangerous to travel.

As food became more scarce, the colonists became more discontent. They argued among themselves, even fought each other. This did nothing to help their cause. It made them weaker and subjected them to more sickness and disease. What could they eat? Some colonists found and ate berries and roots. Others ate insects and mice. Every day was a new task to find enough food.

As Richard felt his empty stomach rolling, he listened to the colonists grumble, becoming more and more discontent. From time to time, they looked at Jack with hunger in their eyes. They spoke of killing one of the few horses for food. This was a very desperate time.

Work on building and repairing parts of the fort stopped. No one had strength enough to lift the tools or move materials. Richard knew things were very bad. They would soon do anything, eat anything, to survive.

Early one morning Richard wrapped a few things in an old shirt and, with Jack, disappeared into the woods. He had a small piece of <u>flint</u> to start a fire and his knife. Also, he carried an axe which could be used to chop wood. No one would miss these things. It could be no worse away from the fort. There were no Indians nearby. Perhaps he could find in the woods some plants, berries or a small animal to eat. And he could protect Jack. He knew they would soon kill and eat him. Richard would rather die than eat his best friend.

At first Richard and Jack walked slowly along the river bank. The wind was cold and damp. They were chilled and stopped to rest often, for they were both weak. At midday they went inland, hunting for anything to fill their empty stomachs. Suddenly Richard heard movement in the trees. He looked up to see a squirrel running down a tree trunk to the ground near his feet. Jack growled as Richard brought the axe down across the squirrel's back, killing it. What good luck — a meal for the two of them!

Richard had never before skinned an animal, but he needed this food. Now, with new energy, he made a fire and began to talk to Jack as he worked.

"What do you think, my friend? Aren't we lucky? That axe came in handy. Let's see, where do I begin on our furry friend? I'll cut off his tail first, and then try to get my knife under the fur to pull it toward his head. I have watched this several times, but not closely. It is quite bloody. Here, Jack, you may nibble on the tail while I work on the rest of him." Slowly Richard worked through the bloody process. He walked back to the river to wash the skinned squirrel. He added twigs to the fire, made a <u>spit</u> from a sharp stick, and began roasting his prize.

Richard and Jack ate slowly, enjoying each bite. How wonderful it felt to have food again! As night approached, they lay near the fire. Richard was planning what to do next.

"There must be other squirrels nearby. Perhaps, just perhaps, we could kill more with this trusty tool and take them back to the fort to share with the others. What do you think, my friend. Well, let's rest now and wait until daylight."

Early the next morning, Richard was awakened by Jack's barking and running about. He quickly looked around in the woods for a deer, a rabbit, or a snake — whatever was disturbing Jack. The sounds of something coming through the woods became louder. It was getting closer and closer. Richard grabbed the axe, his only weapon against attack. Raising it above his head, he stood firmly facing the approaching enemy. Jack continued to bark and run — first toward the sound, then back to his master.

Suddenly through the trees came two figures. "Richard-boy, it's Nate and Sam. Put down your weapon. We've come to take you back. Last night we saw smoke from your fire. At sun-up we set out to find you. Are you okay? You have given us quite a scare!" Nathaniel Peacock and Samuel Collier were two of the boys at Jamestown.

"Speaking of 'scare,' you have given me a good one. I thought you were some wild animals or Indians attacking me!" said Richard.

"We know why you ran away with Jack. You feared he would be killed and eaten," explained Nate. "You were smart. Two dogs were eaten, also a horse. But now Jack will be safe."

"How can you be sure of that?" asked Richard.

"Well, Pocahontas, with several of her natives — all dressed in warm animal skins — came to bring corn and smoked meat," said Sam. "She came for news of John Smith, my master. He was her good friend. Things are better now. No one must eat dogs or horses or snakes."

"Come back with us," urged Nate. "This is no place to survive alone."

The three boys, with Jack at their heels, made their way back to Jamestown and the fort. The two good friends returned home.

HUZZAH, KING JAMES!

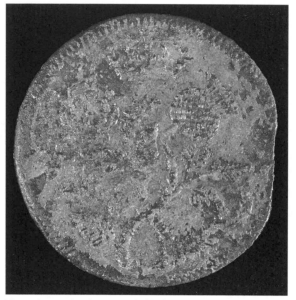

Copper "coins" with an intertwined rose and thistle under a crown are "king's touch" tokens. Several were uncovered during the third year of excavation.

Jamestown Rediscovery III, 1997
Association for the Preservation of Virginia Antiquities

His eyes burned from the smoke of the fire, but John Herd knew he must soon open them and look around to see what remained of his home in the James Fort. Only days ago, Captain Christopher Newport had arrived from England with food and gunpowder, as well as a number of new colonists. This was to be a new day for Jamestown, and now this — another tragic fire. John only hoped the storehouse with the new supplies was safe.

Black ashes covered the ground as, very slowly, one by one, the weary settlers struggled to save some of their belongings. Fire was always a problem in the early days at Jamestown. The blacksmith's <u>forge</u>, the glassmaking oven, the weapons <u>magazine</u> were all spots where fires might begin. Once started, they were hard to stop. During these first months the colonists lost more from fire than from Indian attacks.

Jamestown Island was full of trees. Wood was found throughout the small settlement to build the fort, the church, homes, and tools. There was so much wood the colonists sent lumber back on supply ships to show the <u>Virginia Company of London</u> that a colony in the new world was worth their support. Company leaders had hoped the settlers would find gold and other, more valuable exports, but alas, none had been found.

John Herd was a bricklayer by trade. He spoke often of the need for a better material for building. He could see the value of making bricks from the clay of the river bank. Of course, these bricks would need to be baked in ovens to make them strong — another possibility of fire. There were dangers in everything.

As morning came, John lay on the ground near the spot where he fell after carrying many buckets of river water to help put out the fire. He was near the remains of the <u>longhouse</u> where he slept. He saw that a small part of his sleeping <u>pallet</u> was still there, but in spite of their hours of work, the longhouse had burned to the ground. His arms moved slowly through the ashes, still warm from the fire. He moved his legs. They seemed to be working. As he turned his head to the right, he saw his friend, William Johnson, who was a laborer like John. William was not moving.

"Will, are you alive?" yelled John. "Open your eyes; move your legs. Are you fit?"

"I'm not at all sure," responded William in a whisper. "I seem to have a bad foot. It may be burned or sprained. I can't tell."

"Stay as you are then, mate. I am now up on my knees. I'll crawl over and have a look at you," ordered John.

"Where did the fire start? How did it spread so fast?" asked William.

"My guess is, it started by sparks from a cooking fire, but who knows?" John answered. "Most likely it spread with the wind from the river. How many fires is this, Will, two or three since we arrived?"

"Too many, I'd say," William answered. "We've a lot of rebuilding to do, John."

Fires cost the colonists quite a lot. One of the first destroyed the church and with it the Rev. Robert Hunt's library of books. Books at this time were of great value because so few were printed.

John crawled to inspect his friend's injury. Then wrapping the foot in the cleanest clothing he could find, he helped William to his feet. "Once daylight comes, and we can see a bit better, I'll get you to the surgeon," said John. "For now, rest here against this tree while I try to find our things, if any remain."

As John moved slowly about, he found others searching through the ashes, and still others sick from the smoke or injured from burning tree limbs. He went, once more, to the river to bring water to those in need.

William pushed away from the tree where he sat and, leaning on a strong tree limb, he began hopping on his good foot to help his friends.

"Will," called John, "should you be about on your bad foot? Mr. Wilkinson, our surgeon, will be here soon to look at you and the others. That is, if he himself is up and about."

"Thanks, John, but I am fine with this tree crutch to lean on. I really need to help the others and to look for my own few things. I don't have much, but it is all worth saving."

There was very little food on this day after the fire. Some of the new supplies from Captain Newport's ship were destroyed by fire or water. This was yet another hardship to bear. How could they go on? At times it seemed impossible to build an English colony in this New World.

On hands and knees near their sleeping area, William and John sifted through the ashes. John found his belt buckle; William, his cup and plate. What a sad hunt! They had so little in the first place — and now had so much less. How could they go on?

"There is one small thing I just must find. Surely the fire would not destroy it," muttered John, as his hands moved quickly from place to place.

"What might you be looking for, my friend?" asked William. "There is little here that is not burned to ashes.

"In and of itself, there is no value to this piece," explained John, "but the meaning is most valuable. I am looking for my touch coin, which my mum got for me before we sailed. She must have paid a good quid for it. She believes it had been touched by King James himself and that I should keep it with me at all times for my protection. I really must find it!"

"Of what size is it, John? I have never seen a 'touch coin,'" said William. "Touched by the King, you say? Can you describe it?"

"Well, it is most likely made of copper and is the size of any other money piece. On one side is stamped the rose for England and thistle for Scotland under the King's crown. Mum believes, as do many, that the King has powers of a god and that these powers stay with such coins," explained John. "They protect those who carry them. Look about and help me find it, will you? It was in the pocket of my pants, which I took off at bedtime before the fire."

The two friends worked through the day repairing the outer wall of the fort — their first protection from the Indians. William stopped often to rest his injured foot. The surgeon, Mr. Wilkinson, had cleaned and wrapped it in a proper bandage with ointment from his supplies. William was resting as John continued to look for his coin.

From the storeroom, corn and smoked fish were passed to the hungry settlers. They carefully prepared fires for cooking, placing stones around the blazes. It was quiet inside the James Fort. The men and boys were tired and dazed and sad. They sat in small groups without a sound.

Suddenly, a loud whoop went up from John Herd as he ran into the midst of a group near the site of the longhouse. "I've found it!" yelled

John jumping up and down. "I've found my lucky piece! It was hidden by a rock which I passed by many times today. Who knows how it got there? Here it is, lads! Have a look! Better yet, touch it! Don't ask me how I know, but finding this touch coin will surely bring us good luck and better times. Join me in a cheer for our King — Huzzah! For our King James! Huzzah! May he live a long and healthy life!"

GLOSSARY

artifact – An object found in the ground by archaeologists.

bellows – a tool that is squeezed to force air through a nozzle and fan a fire. Blacksmiths used bellows to keep a fire going, which heated the iron objects they were molding.

blockhouse – part of a military fort made with very strong material used for a lookout.

bodkin – a silver pin meant to be used to decorate a woman's hair as well as hold it in place.

breastplates – a piece of armor that covers the chest area of a soldier.

bulwark – a projection at a corner of a fort where cannons were placed.

carbon-dating – Burned objects turn into carbon. This test can help tell how old something is that was burned.

catalogue – To list each artifact found.

Council – a small group of men that governed the colony.

crucible – a container used for melting materials at very high temperatures.

fishmonger – one who catches and sells fish.

flint – a hard quartz stone that sparks when struck with steel, used to start a fire.

forensic anthropologists – Scientists who learn about past peoples' lives by studying their bones.

forge – a hearth or furnace where metal is heated and then pounded into a shape.

ground radar – A way of detecting hidden objects beneath the ground without digging (disturbing) the ground.

jacks – iron pieces sewn onto vests to be worn for protection somewhat like a breastplate.

litter – a flat framework bed used to carry a wounded person.

longhouse – a long, wooden building built with poles used to store supplies or where many men slept.

Low Countries – a region in Europe made up of Belgium and the Netherlands. Many English soldiers helped fight wars in these countries before coming to Virginia.

magazine – a storehouse where weapons and gunpowder were stored.

matchlocks – muskets fired by a burning fuse.

mum – another word for mother.

muskets – long shoulder guns.

palisade – a wall or fence of a fort.

pallet – a bed of straw or some sort of bedding used on the floor.

patron – a sponsor or someone who supported a person.

pikes – weapons with a metal tip on the end of a wooden pole.

Powhatans – the name of a Native American tribe in eastern Virginia now and in the 17th Century.

quid – British money equal to a pound of sterling.

spit – a long rod onto which meat is put for cooking over a fire.

sturgeon – a very large and tasty freshwater fish.

Thames River – a river that flows through England.

Virginia Company of London – a group of businessmen who, hoping to make a profit, gave money to send colonists to Virginia.

INDEX